Jennifer's Story
Pleasantly Plump – Book 1
Shannon Stiles

Table of Contents

Disclaimer

This book contains adult language and *very* explicit sexual content. It is not intended for nor suitable for anyone under the age of 18, nor for those who find this type of material offensive. If you fall into either of these two categories, please do NOT read this.

"I am *not* fat!" I told my full-length bathroom mirror as I climbed out of the shower. I'd caught it staring at me.

This is the part where, in the movies, the mirror answers back and says something like, "Well, *I* certainly didn't say anything." But my mirror evidently had no acting skills. It just sat there, staring at me, never saying a word.

"I'm soft and curvy, with beautiful, full titties, a nice, round ass, and a pussy that deserves way better than I get from David," I continued, repeating the affirmation I'd written for myself and was now required to repeat at least 10 times a day, according to the online *Pussy Power* course I was taking.

Every word of that affirmation was true. A lot of guys would put me in the category known as *Pretty Fucking Hot*, I was sure. But not David. With him it was always, *Hey, babe, why don't you try to lose a few pounds?* or, *You putting on weight, sweetie?* frequently followed by a slap on the ass.

And all because of an extra five or ten pounds of baby fat. Baby fat! Hell, I'm only 20 years old. In a couple of years that will probably all be gone and I'll be skinny again, just like when I was a youngster. Which is what David wants, apparently – a skinny little wench of a woman!

I've never really understood that. Why some guys are so into screwing those skinny, bony model-types, I mean. That couldn't be a lot of fun for either of them, clanging their hip bones together as they banged away. You'd think those guys would rather be lying on a soft, warm body with a little padding. Like mine.

Anyway, if *wham-bam-thank-you-ma'am* David was doing the screwing, there wasn't much to worry about, I guess. He was seldom in the saddle long enough to do any real damage. That thought brought a smile to my lips as I got dressed, followed by a frown as I realized that's all I ever really got from him – a quickie. David was almost always a quick, unsatisfying fuck, at least for me.

Too bad he couldn't be more like Alejandro. Alejandro knew how to treat a woman, both in and out of bed. He was kind and gentle, as well as being tall, dark and mysterious, muscular, and handsome. And, best of all, perhaps, he was equipped with eight inches of the smoothest, most beautiful, most delicious man-meat possible – a cock that would more than satisfy just about any girl.

Only trouble was, Alejandro wasn't real. He was a sweet vision, existing only in my head, a guy I'd invented years ago. He was the guy I imagined each time I gave my vibrator a workout.

Yeah, my vibrator, my wonderful vibrator. A vibrating dildo, actually. The only time my pussy ever got any real action was when I broke out that old, eight-inch fake cock I bought myself for my nineteenth birthday. I ordered it online and didn't realize how long it was. And *thick*, too. That little jewel took some getting used to – a thick eight inches was a tight fit. But it fits better now, thanks to lots of practice over the past year or so. Which reminded me – I needed to replace it. The silicone was beginning to peel off from overuse.

I'd definitely gotten my money's worth from it, though. Maybe I'll order the six-speed, 10-inch monster dong, this time, I thought. That's the one with the little clit-rubbing extension on one side and a mini-dick sticking out the other side, so you can fuck yourself in the pussy and the ass at the same time, if you want to. I'm not sure I'll be using it that way on a regular basis, but I'll definitely give it a try because I once had a guy stick his finger up my ass while he was pounding my pussy and I came almost immediately. That was one of the best orgasms I ever had!

My phone rang and I picked it up. "Hey, what's up?" I said to my best friend, Marlene. We've been friends since elementary school and she calls me two or three mornings a week at about this time, to "check in," as she phrases it, but I sometimes think she calls me just to see if I'm still alive.

"Wha'cha doin'?" she said.

"Nothing. Getting dressed. Talking to my mirror."

"Yeah? About what?"

"You know – David, guys, the fact that I haven't had a good screwing in over a month. That kind of shit."

Marlene laughed. "I can't believe a dick-friendly girl like you can't find a guy to give her a good fuck."

"What makes you think I'm *that* dick-friendly?"

"You like dicks, don't you?"

"Well, duh! Of course. Where would the world be without dicks?" I said, laughing.

"That makes you dick-friendly. If you like them, you have to be friendly to them."

It was tough to argue with that logic. "I guess." I said.

"So, listen, you wanna go to a flick tonight?"

"Can't. I've got a date with David."

"Oh." Marlene didn't much care for David. Although she'd never actually told me she didn't like him, I could tell from the way she reacted whenever I mentioned him that she thought I could do better.

"Maybe some other night?" I suggested. "This is more like a business meeting than a date. Some college friend of David's is moving here and David wants to help him buy a house, or rent an apartment, or something. So the three of us are going out for drinks." David was a real estate agent, so this was both a business meeting and a college reunion of sorts.

"Yeah, okay. Some other night, then. Anyway, I gotta go. Just wanted to check in."

"I'm still alive," I told her.

"That's good," she said, and hung up.

I finished dressing and headed off to school, where I was already five minutes late for my psych class.

David showed up at eight, right on time, as always. "Ready?" he said.

"Yup. Let's go." I turned off my lights and we headed down the steps to his car.

"You look nice tonight," he said, as he opened the car door and held it for me.

Whoa! What the fuck was that? A compliment from David – I must have misheard him. I've worn this outfit a dozen times before and he's never said a word about it. "Thanks," I said, climbing in. "You look nice, too."

He grinned and closed the door, then got in the other side and we left, heading for – well, I didn't know where we were going. David hadn't mentioned it.

"Where's this friend of yours? I thought he was going to have drinks with us."

"Yeah, he is. Al – that's his name, Al – said he'd meet us there."

Al? Could that be short for Alejandro? I smiled inwardly at the thought. "Where's *there*? Where are we going?" I said.

"Dottie's. I told him we'd meet him there at around eight-thirty."

Of course. Dottie's Den, David's favorite bar and grille. Tiny little tables with tiny little lamps putting out so little illumination you couldn't see the high prices on the menu. Watery drinks, crappy food and rude, snarky servers – what's not to like? Plus, there was an overall *damp* feeling to the place. I hated it.

We got there early – Dottie's was only 10 or 12 blocks from my place. The dining room was pretty much empty, about normal for a weekday night. We skipped through to the lounge, also just about empty, and grabbed a booth with a view of the entrance. I've always wondered how this place stays in business. Every time we've been here it's been like this – empty. Of course, we always come during the week because David is so busy on weekends, what with open houses and stuff. They probably did a shitload of business on weekends, was my guess.

"What's this friend of yours look like?" I said, after we'd ordered and our drinks had come.

"He's tall. Dark. He's from Mexico, I think. Or Colombia. Someplace in South America. Yeah, Colombia, maybe."

"Don't you know? I thought you were friends."

"Yeah, well, more like acquaintances, really. I know him from school and he knows I'm in real estate, so he contacted me."

Hmm. Tall, dark, and Hispanic. Just like Alejandro. I took a big gulp of the illegally-served, watery screwdriver in front of me and began to fantasize about the mysterious Al from Mexico. Or Colombia. Or someplace in South America.

"That's him," David said, interrupting my reverie.

I looked up and practically choked. The large, muscular man walking toward us with a huge smile on his dark face looked almost exactly like my fantasy man – the man who filled my thoughts while I rode my dildo – Alejandro.

Fuck! Was this possible? Maybe I was dreaming. Yeah, that had to be it. I fell asleep on my couch, waiting for David, and now I was dreaming. But I wasn't dreaming, so I stood up, along with David, to greet him.

David introduced us. "Al Entavez, this is my main squeeze, Jennifer," he said.

That really pissed me off. Him calling me his 'main squeeze,' I mean. I wasn't anybody's 'squeeze,' main or otherwise. Least of all David's. David was just a temporary distraction, someone who was supposed to make me happy for a while and then move on. And he wasn't doing a very good job of it.

"Well, *hel-lo*, Jennifer," Al said, taking my hand in his. He stepped back and took a good long look at me, eyeing me from head to toe as David looked on, beaming. A weak feeling slid into my knees.

"David told me he was bringing his girlfriend tonight," Al continued, "but he failed to mention she was a model. A *very* beautiful model." That weak feeling left my knees and slithered up my inner thighs.

"Always the kidder," David commented, sitting back down.

Fuck you, David.

Al was still standing there, holding my hand in his and eyeballing me in a decidedly non-kidding manner. I could feel the warmth creeping up my neck and knew I was blushing, so I did the only thing I could think of. I shook his hand, said, "Thank you for the compliment, Al," and sat back down.

"Call me Alex," he said, sitting down beside me. "I prefer that to Al."

Alex. All right. I'd been hoping that Al was short for Alejandro, but what the hell – Alex was a perfectly nice name. I was also a little disappointed that Alex had no noticeable accent. He sounded like an American. The Alex of my fantasies – whoops, I meant the *Alejandro* of my fantasies – always told me how hot I was in a really sexy Hispanic accent. Oh, well, as the song goes, *You Can't Always Get What You Want.*

David didn't waste any time rehashing their college years or catching up on more recent events in their lives – he got right to work. "So, you're looking for a place here in Orlando, huh? You wanna rent or buy?"

Alex turned his attention away from me and toward the task at hand – finding a place to live. "I guess I'd like to rent for about a year, get used to the community, you know, then buy a place."

"Excellent way to go about it," David said. "I can help you with that."

I sipped my drink and tuned them out, losing myself in fantasies about Alex. Or Alejandro. I wasn't sure which of them I was daydreaming about, since the two men were practically identical, but I was just getting to a good part when David's phone rang, snapping me back to reality.

"What, now?" I heard him say, followed by a period of silence. Then, "Shit, Joan, it's almost nine o'clock. I'm in a bar."

A longer period of silence followed, presumably while Joan, the office manager at David's company, explained whatever had caused this interruption.

"All right, all right. Fifteen minutes," he said, and hung up.

"Something wrong?" Alex said.

"Crap! I'm sorry – I've gotta go to the office."

"Now?" both Alex and I said at the same time.

"Yeah. Look, I'll only be gone a half-hour. I've just gotta sign some papers that need to be delivered by eight o'clock tomorrow morning. Take me two minutes and then I'll come right back. You guys just stay here, have a couple of drinks, get to know one another or whatever, and I'll be back before you know it. Okay?"

Alex tossed a quick, smiling glance in my direction, then turned back to David and said, "Sure. No problem." I nodded my agreement, as if I really had a say in what David intended to do.

"Great, then." He drained his glass, offered us a final, "I'll be back in a jif," and left.

A couple of hours and a few drinks later, David still hadn't returned. Alex and I had taken his advice and had been 'getting to know one another or whatever.' In fact, we'd gotten to know each other so well that Alex's left hand was resting on my right thigh and I was seriously thinking of reaching over and grabbing his dick through his pants. Blame that on the alcohol, I suppose. I'm not usually aggressive around men – I like them to make the first move.

"I'm sorry about David," I told Alex. "Something unusual must have happened and he forgot all about us."

"Fine with me," he said, lightly massaging my inner thigh. No doubt he was testing me, wanting to see if I'd resist his advances – you know, slap his face, act outraged, and say something like, "Just what do you think you're doing?!!"

I *resisted* by spreading my legs apart, giving his hand more room to ... well, to do whatever it was planning to do. The lounge was so dark and uncrowded we probably could have had sex right there in the booth and no one would have noticed. Except – our server was back.

"Get you folks another round?" he said, ogling me. That was probably because I was perspiring and perhaps – just *perhaps* – panting a little bit.

I felt like I should make some excuse to him – explain how it was the booze that was making me look all hot and bothered, not the fact that Alex's fingers had been, and still were, only a couple of inches from my pussy and working their way closer. But I didn't. Instead I said, "It's awfully hot in here tonight," and fanned myself with my hand.

"Yes, ma'am," he said. "Hot." He turned to Alex. "So? Drinks?"

"No, I think we'll be leaving now." Alex left his hand on my thigh and glanced in my direction. "Okay?"

I nodded. "Fine."

"Yeah, we're gonna leave. Just bring us the check, please."

"They keep the tab at the bar. You can settle up at the front."

Alex removed his hand from my thigh, giving it one last long and *very* friendly squeeze. He left a twenty on the table for the server – pretty generous, in my opinion – and we gathered our belongings and headed to the front to settle the tab.

We were about halfway there when David came rushing in, looking slightly panicked.

Shit! David! Nice timing! was my reaction upon seeing him.

"Glad to see you made it back," Alex said. He didn't look glad, in my opinion.

"What happened?" I said. "Why didn't you call?"

"I got arrested."

"What?!"

"Uh, ... not arrested, exactly. Detained. I was coming back here and got pulled over and for the past couple of hours I've been trying to prove that I actually *do* own the car I was driving. Either something was wrong with my registration – that's what the cops said – or it was their fucking tablets. Whatever, by the time we got it all straightened out there were four cop cars there. I felt like a real criminal."

"Well, I'm happy they let you go," I said, not feeling particularly happy, at all. "They *did* let you go, didn't they? You didn't run away, did you?" I giggled slightly at the thought of David fleeing the police.

"Yes, Jen, they let me go," he said. He turned and fixed his gaze on me, looking slightly angry about my little joke. "Shit, Jen, what happened to you, anyway? You're all flushed. You gotta lay off the booze, babe. You know all those calories go straight to your ass!"

Ooh, that's it, asshole! No pussy for you, tonight! I'll find some other way to work off all those calories! I wanted to tell him it was his super-hot friend, Alex, not the alcohol, that was making me look the way I did, but I didn't, of course.

"So, let's go sit back down and continue our discussion," David said to Alex.

"I don't think so. It's kinda late. I'm tired and I have to get up early tomorrow."

"C'mon, just one drink."

"No, I've really had enough. But we can do this another time, if you want."

David looked at me for help. "Convince him to stay, Jen."

Really? And how was I supposed to do that? Drop to my knees and start sucking his cock? 'Cause that's what I felt like doing and I'm pretty sure that would convince him to stay, too.

"I think he's right, David," I said. "It's late. I have an early-morning class tomorrow morning. And we can do this some other time."

"Fine," he said, obviously irritated that I hadn't backed him up. "Another time, then."

David picked up the tab, putting it on his business account, and we left. The ride home was a little tense. Neither of us said a word until we got to my place, when I said, "Thanks for the drinks, David," and hopped out of the car before he could get any romantic ideas. I ran up the steps toward the safety of my apartment and when I was inside, with the door locked, I heard him leave, burning a little rubber as he peeled out of the parking lot.

Good riddance, was my reaction to that – I was glad he was gone. I'd been thinking for some time that our relationship was pretty much over, but had put off doing anything about it. But tonight had been the knife-in-the-back of the David-Jennifer romance. That remark about the calories going to my ass was the final straw. David was about to be moved into the *been there, done that* category.

But first things first. I went online and ordered the ten-inch monster dong, the one with the clit-teasing and butt-fucking extensions and six vibrating speeds. One hundred and nineteen dollars plus another eight bucks for expedited shipping, and worth every fucking penny, according to hundreds of reviews from *extremely* satisfied customers. That done, I crawled into bed with my old, about-to-be-replaced dildo – the one I had long-ago named Alejandro.

"I'm sorry, Alejandro," I said, softly. "You've been wonderful, but in a couple of days I'm going to retire you. A new lover is coming to take your place. I'm not sure what his name is going to be, just yet, but I've been thinking about calling him *Alex*. That's a nice name, don't you think?"

As usual, dildo-Alejandro didn't have much to say.

"Well, *I* like it. In the meantime, how about you and me, you know? Once more for old-time's sake?" I fluffed up my pillow, turned out the light, and made myself comfortable. Maybe, with just a little luck, I could conjure up both Alex *and* Alejandro for tonight's fantasy fuck. A threesome – that sounded like fun!

I slept late on Friday morning. Actually, I'd awakened early and seen that the outside world was overcast and blustery, so I'd decided to slide on my early-morning class and go back to sleep. Also, I was extremely tired from a combination of all the alcohol I'd consumed and the 92 orgasms I'd experienced the night before, thanks to the efforts of fantasy Alejandro and fantasy Alex. (Okay, that last part might be just a *little bit* of an exaggeration!)

Later, after I got up, I found out the reason for the gray skies. A hurricane that had been churning up the Gulf, heading toward the panhandle, had made an unexpected turn to the east at Tampa and was now heading directly for Orlando. Tampa had been wiped out and we were expected to get hit with winds in excess of 80 MPH sometime later that night or early Saturday morning.

The weather dictated that I stay home and catch up on some of my schoolwork – the tons of reading I'd been putting off. After debating with myself about which of the eight books on the assigned reading list I felt like reading, I ended up choosing *Abnormal Sexual Behavior of the South Pacific*, an examination of some of the weird shit Pacific Islanders were into. Sexually, of course.

It was a great book – full of tales of sex orgies on the beach, stories of women who would stuff coconuts up their cunts while they sucked off a line of men, stuff like that. Most of it sounded like fun, not that abnormal at all, with the possible exception of that coconut thing. I wasn't in any great hurry to try that!

One of the things I really liked about the book was that it made my own, so-called *abnormal* sexual desires seem so much more *normal*. And what would those be, you say? Well, for one thing, I like big cocks. Long ones. And thick, too. That's my preference – long, thick dicks that give a girl that *full* feeling as they slide in and out of her juicy pussy. I love that feeling!

There's another weird thing I like, too, and I've never told anyone about this, not even Marlene. I love the taste of cum. It's delicious. Not only do I love the taste of it, but the feel of it, too, as that rich, creamy goodness explodes out of a cock, into my mouth, and slides down my throat. Technically, according to much of the literature I've read, that officially makes me a *pervert*.

As the afternoon wore on and the wind began to pick up, I found myself growing sleepy again. The groaning of the wind as it blew through the huge oak tree outside my apartment had an almost hypnotic effect on me. I put down the book, turned off the light, closed my eyes and leaned back against the couch.

I soon found myself in a fantasy involving myself, Alejandro, Alex, and a beach – a beautiful, white-sand beach with tiny, turquoise waves lapping at our feet and dolphins playing in the surf. We were naked, of course, and I had a huge, rock-hard cock in each hand, trying to decide which one I wanted in my pussy and which one I wanted in my mouth. And then, just as I was about to make up my mind, I looked up and saw David, also naked, running down the beach toward us, carrying ... what was that, anyway? A coconut?

David! Fuck! Where did he come from? He wasn't supposed to be part of this fantasy. If he thought he was going to join our little menage a trois on the sand and turn it into a menage a quatre, he was wrong, wrong, wrong!

As far as I was concerned, my relationship with David was a done deal. Over. Kaput. A cooked turkey. Or something to that effect. And that included fantasies. I was fed up with him calling me fat and treating me as if I *was* fat. Like that shit with the alcohol last night. Calories going to my ass, indeed. My ass was just fine, thank you.

Both dicks went limp in my hands as I then proceeded to go on a 10-minute-long internal rant listing all the things I didn't like about the way David treated me, ending with the fact that he'd just ruined my pleasant afternoon fantasy. And what did he think he was going to do with that coconut, anyway? I didn't really want to know.

I sat up and turned on the light as Alejandro and Alex and their no-longer-hard cocks faded away, taking the beautiful beach and David with them. *Thanks a lot, David,* I thought. *You're a piece of shit even in a fantasy!*

The wind was blowing even harder, now, and it was pretty dark, even though it was only about five in the afternoon. It looked as if the hurricane would soon be upon us. I wondered if there was anything I was supposed to do, some hurricane precautions that would keep me safe from the expected wind. Even if there were, it was probably too late. For better or worse, I was stuck in the top-floor apartment of this two-story wood-framed duplex.

My phone rang. I didn't recognize the number but it was local. I debated whether to answer – it was probably just a robocall trying to sell me a prepaid funeral plan. Or not. Maybe it was the lottery calling to tell me I won. That wasn't a call I wanted to miss. So I answered.

"Jennifer?" said the voice on the other end.

I recognized it immediately. "Alex? Is that you?" I said, wondering how he got my number – had David given it to him?

"Yes." He paused. "I hope I'm not bothering you but –"

"You're not bothering me," I said, cutting him off. "Not at all." *Unless you mean it in the sense of 'all hot and bothered,' in which case, then, yeah*, I thought, smiling to myself.

"Great. Well, I was thinking about you. And this storm that's coming. Are you all right? Are you *going* to be all right?"

Wow. He's been thinking about me. And I've been thinking about him, too. What a coincidence. "Yeah, I guess so. I hope so. As long as this place of mine doesn't blow away in the wind, I'll be fine."

"Is that likely to happen? Are you in danger?"

"No, probably not," I said.

"Probably?"

"Well, I'm a student, you know. I'm not rich. I live in the kind of place a student can afford – it's older, it's wood, not really strong like concrete or anything like that."

"I see. Um, … I was wondering, would you like to come over to my place and wait out the storm?"

"Your place?"

"My hotel, I mean. It's concrete. Very sturdy. Plus, there's a wonderful lounge on the 10th floor. We could have drinks, you could teach me about Orlando – I understand you grew up here."

"I did."

"So?

"Well, …" I was dying to accept his invitation but I didn't want to appear *too* eager.

"It's settled then. I'll have my driver pick you up."

Driver? He has a driver? "All right, I guess. Give me some time, okay? Maybe around eight?"

"Wonderful. I can't wait to see you."

"You know where I live?" I said.

"I do," he said.

Paul, Alex's driver, picked me up at precisely eight o'clock in a big, black Mercedes limousine. Local limos cruising our streets are pretty common here but this one was a cut above the rest – what Marlene would have described as, "soo-pah!"

I sat in the back, which had a bar, a computer station and a TV – none of which I made use of – as we wound our way through rain-slick streets toward a part of town unfamiliar to me. The wind had picked up considerably. Shortly before I left, local news had reported gusts as high as 47 MPH. The rain, though, was intermittent, as the outer bands of the approaching storm swept across the city at 10-15 minute intervals.

I wasn't really worried much about the storm. I grew up here, in Orlando, and I'd been through lots of hurricanes and tropical storms. Since the city was inland, well away from both coasts, storms usually lost much of their strength before they hit us, and we seldom suffered any major damage. Still, it's always better to be prepared, they say.

And I *was* prepared – for Alex. I'd spent the time between his phone call and his limousine's arrival taking a long bath and carefully shaving my pussy until it was as smooth as a glass table top. It wouldn't do for Alex to scratch his face on some stray stubble down there, if you know what I mean. After a short debate with myself on whether or not to wear panties, I'd slipped them on and then added the sexiest outfit I could put together. When I'd checked myself in the mirror, only one word came to mind – hot!

Of course, all that effort could be for nothing. Maybe I was misjudging the situation, and what had happened between Alex and me at the bar last night was due solely to the large amount of alcohol consumed. Perhaps he even wanted to apologize for, you know, that inner thigh massage he'd given me. I certainly hoped that wasn't going to happen. I'd *liked* that.

You know what's gonna happen, whispered that little voice in my head. But, of course, that wasn't true – I only knew what I *wanted* to happen!

Alex was waiting for me when we arrived. Apparently Paul had notified him in some fashion of our imminent arrival, although I hadn't heard him make a call or anything like that. Maybe they were telepathically linked, I thought, smiling to myself at the ridiculousness of that idea.

"I'm so glad to see you again," he said, grinning broadly and holding the door open as he helped me out of the car. He was dressed casually – Bermuda shorts, a polo shirt and ratty-looking white sneakers with no socks.

"I'm glad to see you, too," I said.

My, aren't we formal, commented my inner voice.

The hotel wasn't quite what I'd expected – not one of those big, glitzy touristy places, painted a multitude of colors. It was medium-sized – maybe 15 or 16 stories – and a muted brown in color, located on a quiet street in a neighborhood far from downtown. I supposed this was what people meant by the term *business hotel.*

"C'mon, let's get inside, out of this wind," Alex said. He took my hand and led me through the wide front doors into the lobby. Except for a few employees busily engaged in hurricane preparations, it was relatively empty. Most guests were probably in their rooms, hunkered down, waiting to see what the storm was going to do.

As we walked through the lobby toward the elevators, a couple of employees greeted Alex by name, calling him *Mr. Entavez,* and nodding respectfully in my direction. *Not bad for a guy who's only been in town for a couple of days,* I thought. *He's probably a big tipper.*

"I thought we'd start with a couple of drinks," Alex said when we were on the elevator and headed for the 10th floor. "The lounge here is pretty nice. It's quiet."

<u>*Start*</u> *with a couple of drinks? Start what, Alex?* I knew the answer to that question and it made me smile, but he didn't see it.

Alex was right – the lounge was nice. Small, but nice. It looked as if it was designed for serious drinking and intimate interludes. It was dark, with a bar on the left for drinkers and booths in the back for lovers. There were also a few small tables near the bar, barely large enough to hold a round of drinks.

The booths faced away from the bar and toward a large window, from which you could now see trees dancing in the wind. Everything about the place was perfect, except for the tables. I doubt anyone ever sat at those dinky little tables. They were just too small.

A bar employee – an elderly bald man with a big, bushy mustache – came forward and greeted us as we entered. "Good evening, Mr. Entavez," he said. "And how are we, this less-than-fine evening?"

"I'm good, Raymond. How about yourself?"

"Also good, sir." He smiled and turned his attention to me. Since I wasn't legally old enough to drink, I'd never been in this exact situation before and didn't know introductions at lounges were required. Or maybe he just wanted me to show him my ID. I didn't know quite what to say or do.

Alex rescued me. "This is my friend, Jennifer," he told Raymond. "We're, … uh, looking for a place to ride out the storm."

"Of course, sir," he said. And then to me, "Hello, Jennifer. Welcome to the Gilford Arms."

I smiled at him and said, "Hello, Raymond."

He led us to one of the booths in the back. I'd figured we'd be sitting back there, once I'd seen the layout of the place. Sitting at the bar wasn't very romantic and I was pretty sure Alex had something like that on his mind. Romance, I mean. And the tables, of course, were out. Way too small.

I ordered a Tom Collins and Alex told Raymond to bring him 'the usual,' which turned out to be some whiskey drink I'd never heard of and couldn't pronounce properly. Probably the national drink of Colombia, was my guess.

We sat there, watching the storm through the window, and made small talk. *Awkward* small talk. You know, the kind where you both know why you're there and each of you is waiting for the other to get things going, to be the one who says, "C'mon, let's go somewhere and fuck."

That didn't happen. Instead, after a short while, Alex said, "Are you hungry?"

As if on cue, my stomach growled. Busted. I couldn't lie my way out of this, so I laughed and said, "Well, ... now that you mention it ..."

Alex grinned. "Let me get you something to eat," he said. "What would you like?"

"They serve food here?"

"No, but I can have them bring us something up from the restaurant downstairs."

"Really?"

"Uh-huh, really." He kept grinning at me, as if he knew something I didn't. "Anything at all, as long as it's steak, ribs, lobster – that's about all they have."

"Lobster?" My mouth began to water – I *love* lobster!

"Yeah. Oh, they have the best lobster rolls. Piled high with huge chunks of lobster on a golden toasted bun. They're the best."

I don't think I was actually drooling but the inside of my mouth was certainly filling up with moisture. I swallowed and said, "That sounds good."

"Lobster it is, then," Alex said. He took out his phone and called the restaurant. When they answered, he said, "Hey, Fred, this is Alex. I'm upstairs in the lounge with my friend, Jennifer, and we're hungry. I'd like a couple of lobster rolls sent up – the big ones."

Silence followed while Alex listened to what Fred had to say. I imagined Fred wasn't all that happy about receiving a call from someone telling him to make *and deliver* a late-evening snack, but after listening for a bit, Alex laughed and said, "Thanks, Fred. You're the best. Pile them high with extra meat and hurry! We're hungry!" He laughed again and hung up, saying, "Be here in a jiffy," to me.

When you have a lot of money, that's the way it works, I guess. You get whatever you want because you can pay for it. And it was pretty obvious by this time that Alex had tons of money, what with the car and the driver and the way everyone in this hotel treated him. Still, it was just a little odd that he could call up the hotel kitchen and tell some guy named Fred to send us up a couple of lobster rolls. And then tell him to make sure to add extra lobster. It must be really nice to be *that* rich!

The lobster rolls were, as Alex had said, 'the best.' Huge. The biggest I'd ever seen. Delicious, of course. I'm sure even people from Maine would have been impressed. And they were delivered by Fred, himself, introduced to me as the manager of the restaurant, which was on the third floor.

From the way they chatted with each other, you'd think Alex and Fred were old friends. That's the way everyone in this hotel treated Alex, it seemed. Like an old friend. This was probably the friendliest hotel in Orlando.

With the lobster rolls devoured and my stomach silenced, we went back to our drinks, small talk, and watching the storm. Alex didn't have much to say. He let me do most of the talking while he watched me, a half-smile on his lips. That was nice. A guy who could shut up and let me talk once in a while – something of a rarity, in my experience.

The wind continued to blow, the trees continued dancing, and the rain was heavier than it had been, but still following it's off-and-on pattern. The outside world looked cold and nasty through the big window, but inside, where we were, things seemed snug and cozy. The alcohol probably had a lot to do with the warm glow I was feeling throughout my body, I assumed.

I told Alex about Orlando and my life growing up here. He probably wanted to know more about the city than about me, but what he got was a mini-recap of my life. I regaled him with stories of past hurricanes I'd experienced, how a dog chased me and bit me on the leg when I was in the third grade, and about the band that played at my junior prom – stupid stuff like that. I blamed the alcohol for that, too.

At about 10 o'clock, the lights in the lounge flickered and then went out. They came right back on again, though, blinked a couple of times and then settled into a soft glow that wasn't quite as bright as it had been. Apparently the hotel had it's own power source.

Raymond came by and told us the lounge was going to close early so the employees could get home before the brunt of the storm hit. From my point of view, it was a strange conversation. For one thing, Raymond was extremely apologetic, as if he were personally responsible for the early closing. He kept saying things like, *I'm <u>so</u> sorry, Mr. Entavez. It's the storm. There's nothing we can do. I'm <u>so</u> sorry,* and Alex kept responding with comments like, *Don't worry about it, Raymond, it's not your fault,* and *Go on home before the storm hits. Be safe.* It was almost as if they were friends, or perhaps long-time acquaintances.

We finished our drinks and left the lounge. The employees were busy doing some last-minute cleaning up, but many of them stopped what they were doing to say goodbye and to wish us luck with the storm. That was nice. It made me feel like a celebrity. It was funny, though, how many of the lounge employees knew Alex by name.

I wondered where we were going, now that the lounge was closed, but to tell the truth, I didn't really care. Just standing there, waiting for the elevator, with Alex's arm around my waist and the warmth of the alcohol coursing through my body, I was as happy as I'd been in a long, long time. "Where are we going?" I said.

"My room."

Of course. His room. That's why I was here, after all. To avail myself of a safe place to stay during the storm. Right.

But as we rode the elevator up toward Alex's room, I began having paranoid thoughts. This really wasn't like me, at all. Going to a strange man's hotel room when I knew the only real reason for me being there was to fuck him silly, I mean. That wasn't something I did – ever! But then, Alex wasn't really a 'strange man' – I knew him. At least, a little bit. And he wasn't just some random fuck, either. He was the walking, talking embodiment of my fantasy lover, Alejandro. In my mind, that made everything A-Okay!

So that's why we're here? You're gonna screw this guy? said the little voice in my head, joining the internal discussion I was having.

Several times, hopefully, I replied.

Are you sure that's what you want to do?

Pretty sure.

He's gonna think you're a slut if you let him fuck you on the first date.

I know, I know. But I wanna.

You could wait. Act like a lady.

I don't wanna wait. I wanna get laid now. Tonight!

You're certain of that?

Yes. I. WANT. TO. FUCK. HIM!

"Did you say something?" Alex said, snapping me back to the here and now.

Did I say that out loud? Shit! I hope not. "No, just a big sigh," I said.

He grinned and said, "Uh-huh," and let it go at that.

Alex's room was on the top floor, but calling it a room was a major insult. It was a suite – gigantic in size, nearly twice as large as my apartment and about five times as nice. A big, brick fireplace took up most of one wall, although it wasn't real. It used gas and fake logs. I knew that because when we entered, Alex turned it on with a remote control and foot-high flames instantly appeared.

Facing the fireplace was a curved sectional with a small refrigerator occupying the center section. Very convenient, I thought when I saw it. No need to get up and get a drink from the kitchen if the heat from the fire made you thirsty.

"Wow, this place is fabulous," I said, taking it all in and at the same time wondering just how much a suite like this cost per night.

"Yeah, it's nice. I always stay here when I'm in town."

"When you're in town?"

"Uh-huh."

"Oh, I thought this was your first time here."

"No, I've been here several times in the past six months or so. Usually just for a couple of days at a time. I'm planning to move here permanently, though."

Oh, so that's why everyone at the hotel knew who he was. "I heard," I said.

We sat close together on the sectional. Alex adjusted the flames so they were just barely visible, flickering above the fake logs. Fireplaces in Florida are mainly for show – it seldom gets cold enough to need them for heat.

"Comfortable?" he said.

"Very." It was true. I felt very comfortable sitting there with Alex, just the two of us, alone without cares or worries, as if we were the only two people in the world. It was as if I'd known him for years and, in a way, I had. Only, his name used to be Alejandro. That was just a minor detail, though.

Outside, the noise of the wind had increased dramatically. I could hear other noises, too, off in the distance – like someone's garbage pail or lawn furniture tumbling down a wind-blown street far away. I couldn't have cared less about any of that. The whole city of Orlando could have blown away by now and it wouldn't have bothered me a bit. I had other things on my mind. I leaned over and rested my head on Alex's left shoulder.

I'm not exactly sure which one of us made the first move but it might have been me, considering the position in which I soon found myself. Alex had slid down a bit, until much of his body was nearly horizontal. I was sitting astride him, pinning him down, so that only his face looked forward, and I was busily engaged in covering it with kisses, which he seemed to enjoy. I know I was enjoying it. After so long doing this same thing with Alejandro in fantasy land, I was now getting to do it for real with Alex.

Sitting there, straddling his lap, I could feel his dick, rock-hard, poking me in the ass, and I wondered if the next move was up to me. Was it? What would he do if I stopped kissing him, slid down, pulled out his dick and, you know, *introduced* myself to it?

I didn't have time to make a decision about that. He looked up at me and said, "C'mon, let me show you the bedroom. You're gonna like that."

I'll bet I am! I thought as I clambered off both him and the sectional and let him lead me by the hand into the bedroom. *I'll just bet I am!*

The bedroom was luxurious, although not as big as I'd thought it would be. It was dimly lit but one feature stood out – a king-sized bed, right in the center of the room, with what I thought was a king-sized mirror mounted directly overhead. I later found out the mirror was actually a king-sized TV. And I know, technically that's *two* features. So sue me.

"Try the bed," Alex said. "It's really soft and comfortable."

Now, this is the part where a lot of girls would pretend to be all shy and bashful and bat their eyelashes and say something like, "Oh, I couldn't. It wouldn't be right," or some such nonsense. Not me. I kicked off my sandals, hopped up onto the bed, slid over and patted the spot next to me. "Come on. Try it with me," I said.

Alex obliged. He joined me on the bed and in no time at all we were back to what we'd been doing in the other room, before we came in here – making out. The only difference was that I was no longer on top. We were more or less side by side, and his right hand was massaging my breasts.

His hand reached up and pulled the spaghetti straps of my blouse down over my shoulders, then tugged my blouse down. I sneaked a peek at my boobs. Oh, no! Did I forget to wear a bra? Too late now, I realized, as I watched Alex lightly caressing my nipples with his lips, making me shiver in anticipation of what lay ahead.

He looked up and me and smiled, then took my right breast in his hand and began gently, well, ... nursing, alternately sucking and swirling his tongue around my nipple, which got so hard it would have made a porn star proud. I don't think babies do that, though, when they nurse. Swirl their tongues around their mom's nips, I mean.

He smiled at me again and made a loud, smacking sound as he released the nipple of my right breast from his lips and headed for the left, apparently with the same intent.

Damn! Were those my nipples, sticking out like that? I've never seen them that big!

This seemed like as good a time as any to show Alex I wasn't here to play games. I slid my hand down and unbuttoned the top button of his shorts, then slipped my hand inside, searching for his dick. It wasn't difficult to find, actually – it was waiting for me, stiff and erect, just past the waistband of his boxers. I wrapped my fingers around it and gave it a friendly *Hi! How are you?* squeeze.

He shuddered. I smiled and continued massaging his cock, milking it just a little, which made him moan. It was a fine cock, in my estimation – big and firm and smooth and seemingly well-prepared for the evening's activities ahead of it. Of course, I hadn't seen it yet and you can't really judge a cock until you've had a good look at it. I could hardly wait for that.

I popped my boob out of Alex's mouth and slid down a bit, at the same time pulling his shorts and boxer shorts down over his knees and off. And there it was, standing firm and erect in the dim light of the room and looking absolutely gorgeous. I stared at it and smiled. It was exactly as I'd imagined it all those times with Alejandro – the cock of a girl's dreams. At least, of *my* dreams.

I rolled over so that I was between Alex's legs. That big, beautiful dick was about two inches from my face, dancing around like the trees outside in the wind. I leaned forward and lightly kissed the head, using just my lips – no tongue – and said, "Hello, there, beautiful. We meet at last." And then I giggled.

A smiling Alex looked down at me, moaned, and said, "Fuck, Jen! Don't giggle. Suck!"

So I sucked. I grabbed the shaft and pulled the head into my mouth, putting my tongue to work, just as I had in all those imaginary sessions with my fantasy-lover, Alejandro. I swirled my tongue around Alex's dickhead, first clockwise, then reversing direction, while I pretended to be a vacuum cleaner.

He seemed to like what I was doing, judging by the way he was bouncing and bucking around, so I slid my mouth down one side of his dick, gave his balls a quick greeting, and then slowly ran my tongue up the bottom of his shaft, from balls to head. Along the way, I added slurping sounds, just to show him how enthusiastic I was about what I was doing.

He *really* seemed to like that, judging by the way his cock jerked awkwardly back and forth in appreciation, so I repeated the maneuver a couple of times.

"Ohhhh, fuck!" he said. "I'm gonna cum!"

"Excellent," I told him, breaking some stupid rule about not talking with your mouth full. That's exactly what I wanted – to feel that little explosive blast from the end of his dick and to taste that warm, delicious baby gravy as it spurted into my mouth and down my throat. I turned my vacuum cleaner up to *high* – the serious sucking setting – and went back to work, adding a little hand action for extra emphasis.

Alex was not a liar. When he said he was going to cum, I mean. Because that's what happened. He reached down, grabbed me by the ears and pulled my head forward so that the tip of his dick was scraping the back of my throat. And then he unloaded a massive torrent of jizz.

I sucked, I swallowed, and I sucked some more. The cum kept coming, spurt after spurt after spurt, shooting into my mouth and surging down my throat while Alex moaned, swore, and twitched. I hadn't known it was possible for a guy to pump out that much cum in one load – it must have been a long time since he got laid.

And then something I'd never heard of and had never experienced took place. His cock, now completely drained thanks to my superior sucking skills, stayed stiff. While I didn't have *that* much experience in draining dicks with my mouth – it wasn't my *specialty*, or anything like that – I was under the impression that once you sucked the last drop of cum from a guy's dick, it was supposed to relax. Go limp. Fall over and play dead, at least for a little while. That was the proper etiquette.

Alex's dick was obviously a rebel, however, and refused to play by the rules. It remained as rigid as it had been before my mouth ever touched it, back when I was warming it up with my hand. I was a little confused but I knew one thing – there was still a stiffy in my mouth and that demanded action. I went back to work, lightly sucking and caressing his dickhead with my tongue.

At some point during all this, my clothes disappeared. I'm not sure exactly how or when that happened – maybe they just wandered off by themselves – but I was now completely naked. And just in time, too.

Alex squirmed around until he'd rotated 180 degrees beneath me, then lifted me up by the hips and planted my crotch directly over his face. I held on tight to his dick and kept sucking as he reached up, placed both hands on my butt and pulled me down so that my pussy was so close to his mouth I could feel his hot breath blowing on it as he breathed.

Take a deep breath, Alex. You're gonna need it! I thought. I reached down, spread apart my pussy lips and planted my moist, juicy cunt directly onto his waiting mouth.

Alex wasn't exactly inexperienced in this particular activity. His tongue – just the tip of it, actually – began slowly sliding up and down that wet slit of mine, lapping up every bit of pussy juice it could find. And there was a *lot* of it – my cunt was practically *dripping!* Each time his tongue reached the top, it circled my clit several times before heading back down. My little love button was bigger and firmer than it had ever been and was enjoying every second of Alex's magic mouth. It was now my turn to buck and moan, and I did!

Alex eventually brought the rest of his tongue into play. And his lips, too. He sucked my clit into his mouth and enveloped it with his tongue, lapping and licking and slurping and sipping and swallowing. I twitched and twerked and shuddered as wave after wave of mini-orgasms swept over me, but I forced myself to wait for the big one I knew would soon be coming.

Temporarily releasing his dick from my mouth, I turned my head back to where he was hard at work, and said, "That feels *soooo good!*" That might have been the understatement of all time – saying it felt *soooo good* really didn't do justice to what I was feeling.

He answered back, talking directly into my pussy, saying something that sounded like, "Yufung nussy ase trate, zen!" in a muffled voice. I was pretty sure that meant, "Your fucking pussy tastes great, Jen!" so I said,

"Glad you like it," popped his dick back into my mouth and resumed tonguing the head.

It seemed as if he was getting ready to cum again. His cock throbbed with every lick I laid on it and the intensity of his moaning increased. He didn't say much, mostly just, "Oh, oh, oh!" and, "Oh, fuck!" but that was okay. I wasn't looking for praise – I knew he liked what I was doing.

He didn't warn me this time, at least not verbally. But the jerking and spasming of his dick tipped me off to what was about to happen. I got ready to take another huge load.

And huge it was! I couldn't believe it – not after what had happened just a few minutes ago. It seemed unlikely that Alex could have *any* cum left for me after the massive load with which he'd already gifted me. But he did. It poured out of his dick, not quite as stupendously mouth-filling as his previous, no doubt record-breaking delivery – that probably would have been impossible, considering the circumstances. But it was still a top-ten contender.

Only slightly surprised by the size of this second load, I lapped it all up, swallowed, and kept sucking. I was curious. Could Alex still keep that beautiful dick of his hard after all it had been through so far?

The answer was no, he couldn't. This time it behaved like a normal cock and shrank. It gave up, surrendered, waved the white flag, lay down and, judging by its actions, seemed to imply it was satisfied. At least, temporarily. That was the way things were supposed to work.

Not wanting to get my pussy *too* excited, I pulled it away from his mouth, rolled off him and flopped over onto my back, still holding his dick in my hand.

Alex looked at me and smiled. "Rest, Jen. Rest," he said.

I smiled up at the TV, where I could just make out a dim reflection of the two of us, lying naked on the bed. *Oh, no, Alex. I'm not the one who needs to rest – it's you. We're just getting started and it's going to be a long night!*

We lay there for a time without talking, just panting, catching our breath and resting. After a while, Alex propped himself up on one elbow and, with a serious look on his face, said, "I hope you don't think I'm a buddy-fucker, Jen."

Buddy-fucker? That was a new one on me. "What's a buddy-fucker?" I asked him. We were still lying feet to head, so I grabbed a pillow and placed it under my head, the better to see him, while I continued to massage his cock with one hand.

"That's a guy who steals his buddy's girl. He fucks over him so that makes him a buddy-fucker."

"I see. And is that what you think you're doing? Stealing me away from David?"

"Well, ... you are his girl."

"Not any more. That ended last night. I just haven't told him yet."

"Really?" He smiled. "Then that's two reasons that make me feel better about tonight, about you and me, you know ..."

"Two? What's the other one?"

"David and I aren't really buddies. We're more like acquaintances. I knew him in college but we didn't hang out together or anything. So when I found out he lived here and sold real estate, I gave him a call."

"That makes you an acquaintance-fucker, then, not a buddy-fucker."

The smile – still on his face – turned into a grin. "I can live with that," he said.

We rested some more while I continued to diddle his dick and think about the possibility that Alex was stealing me away from David. I hoped it was true – that my fantasy-lover would become my real lover. And not for just a one-night stand, either. I was looking for a more permanent relationship.

Meanwhile, his cock had regained some of its earlier enthusiasm and was gradually growing in size. *More good times soon to come, Jen,* commented my inner voice and I sent a message back, *I'm ready!*

Lying there, playing with his dick, it dawned on me that I really didn't know much about Alex. In fact, I didn't know anything at all about him, other than that he was tall and handsome, just like my fantasy-lover, Alejandro, and looked almost exactly as I had pictured him. And I was satisfied with that, at least for tonight!

Of course, there were a couple of other things I knew, too. Like the fact that he was a friend of David's. Whoops! Make that – *acquaintance of David's.* And that he was undoubtedly rich. Maybe even super-rich. But I didn't really care about that. Him being rich, I mean. My interest in Alex wasn't motivated by money. It was something else, entirely. He was my fantasy dream-lover, come to life!

Still, it would be nice to know a little more about him, I thought. So I said, "Alex, can I ask you a personal question?"

"Sure, Jen. Anything."

"How come you don't have an accent?"

"What? Why would I have an accent?"

"Well, you're from ... where? Colombia?"

"Yeah."

"Don't people there have accents?"

He looked puzzled. "I guess some do. But I went to school up north, you know, so I guess mine disappeared."

Now I was confused. I didn't know you could get rid of a Hispanic accent just by spending time 'up north.' I propped myself up on one elbow and stared at him. "Don't they speak Spanish?"

"In Columbia? Not really. Most everyone speaks English."

"They do?" That was a surprise. I thought almost every country in South America spoke Spanish. Except maybe Brazil. "But you're Hispanic, right?"

"Oh, yeah. One hundred percent. Alejandro Juan Entavez, that's me. As Hispanic as you can get."

I sat up. "What? What did you just say?"

"That's my name – my *real* name. Alejandro Juan. I'm named after my grandfather. Alex is just my nickname."

"Holy SHIT!" I said, really loud.

Alex sat up next to me. "What's wrong?" he said, a look of concern on his face.

"It's, ... it's, ... it's your name. Alejandro."

"What's wrong with it?"

"Nothing," I said, clambering forward and kissing him. "It's perfect. Absolutely fucking perfect."

I guess that's when we got back down to serious business. Alex pulled me down on top of him and, in one motion, kissed me and rolled me over, so that he was lying half on top of me and half beside me. His hand slid down to my pussy and he started stroking it, sliding his middle finger slowly up and down, gradually working it inside. Against very little resistance, I might add.

Holy shit! I'm getting finger-fucked by my fantasy-lover! Except, he's no longer a fantasy, and neither is this – this is <u>real</u>! is what I was thinking while all this was going on. And then that little voice in my head got involved.

You're now officially a first-class slut, it said.

No I'm not! I'm not even a second-class slut. I'm a good girl – practically a virgin, by today's standards.

You're sure?

Absolutely.

Well, okay. Have a good time, then.

I will. I am. I'm having the time of my life, I explained to the little voice, but I think it was laughing and didn't hear me.

So, maybe I was a bit of a slut. At least on this night, anyway. I blamed it on the hurricane. If it hadn't been for the hurricane, none of this would have happened. I'd be at home, by myself, maybe studying or watching TV. And Alex would be doing whatever he did when I wasn't around to suck his cock and keep him entertained. Of course, there was also the fact that Alex was the spitting image of Alejandro. That might have been partly to blame. But then, you can't really blame a girl for taking advantage of a once-in-a-lifetime opportunity, can you?

Speaking of Alex, he was between my legs now. My knees were bent up and he'd spread my legs apart. I lifted my head to get a better view of what was going on just as he bent down and ran his tongue up my insanely-wet slit, lapping up every bit of pussy juice he could find. And I was *juicy!*

I said, "OHHHHHH!! Oh! Oh! OH!"

"You like that, do you Jen?" he said, adding a few more licks.

Fuck, yeah, I like it! This was just like being in a porn video. Make-believe Alejandro and I had watched a few of them online – okay, to be truthful, it was actually just me and there were a *lot* of them. I liked watching them. There was a formula to them, a more-or-less logical progression. They always started with a blowjob and then, in the good ones, anyway, threw in a little pussy eating and maybe some fingering before moving on to fucking.

And fuck they did, in so many different positions I couldn't remember the names of them all. But I knew the important ones – *missionary, doggy-style, cowgirl, reverse cowgirl.* There were others, of course, but most of them looked pretty uncomfortable, at least for the girl. I hoped Alex's dick wouldn't wear out before we got to try some of the more-popular positions.

Anyway, I figured we'd be starting in *missionary* position, which is where most of those videos began. And we did, sort of. Alex pulled me forward so that his cock was resting on my pussy. Using his hand to guide it, he then began gently sliding the shaft back and forth along that wet, eager slash between my legs, occasionally just dipping the head in a half-inch or so and then pulling it right back out to continue its journey. I'm sure you've heard the term, *cock-teaser* and know what it means. Alex was just like that – a bit of a *cunt-teaser.* And he was very, very good at it.

I moaned. I groaned. I gasped. Alex's dick, slip-sliding its way back and forth along the pussy path, was about to drive me over the edge. I found myself agreeing with my little voice – I *was* a slut! *Put it in Alex. Stick it in*, I silently pleaded.

I thought that's what he was about to do and I was ready. I could hardly wait to feel the fullness of his big, beautiful – dare I say *magical?* – cock slipping into my juicy, eager pussy. But that's not what happened.

Instead of filling me with dick and happiness, Alex rolled over onto his back, next to me, and said, "Climb aboard, Jen." He lay there, smiling at me, his dick sticking straight up in the air. It was hard to believe – I'd already drained that monster twice, yet there it was, still stiff and erect, like a flagpole. A big, thick flagpole, inviting me to be the flag.

Fortunately, because of all those porn videos I'd watched, I knew exactly what to do. I scrambled to my hands and knees, swung one leg up and over Alex and lowered myself slowly all the way down to the base of the flagpole, just resting there while I adjusted to the deliciously *full* feeling that flagpole riding provides.

So we'd skipped over *missionary* and gone straight to the *cowgirl* position. Or maybe it was *reverse cowgirl* – I'm never quite sure which is which. Anyway, I was on top, face to face with a smiling Alex, and I felt *large and in charge*, as the expression goes. I leaned forward and rocked my body back and forth, sliding that big pole in and out of my wet, slippery pussy.

And that's when I lost it. I'd been holding back so far, content with those little mini-orgasm, but right now my pussy was having none of that. I leaned even more forward, burying my face into Alex's shoulder and began pumping my pussy wildly up and down on Alex's cock. Over and over I lifted myself up slowly and then forcefully plunged back down to the base.

I lasted less than 30 seconds. Thirty seconds of bliss as my long-time fantasy turned into reality. I was fucking my dream guy, my fantasy lover, Alejandro. And that thought was the end of me. I exploded into a shuddering, shaking, shrieking, screaming, screeching, squealing orgasm, bucking and grinding and heaving and twitching until I finally collapsed against Alex, just resting on top of him while I enjoyed a prolonged moment of pure *bliss*.

We lay there in silence for a minute or so, and then Alex commented, "Well, that was impressive."

"Umm," I agreed, although 'impressive' wasn't really a strong-enough word to describe what had just happened. In fact, it was probably impossible to put into words what a glorious feeling it had been, sliding up and down Alex's flagpole. On a scale of one to five, it felt like a fifteen! The fuck-gods, sitting up there in the sky somewhere watching all this, must have taken pity on me and gifted me with this once-in-a-lifetime, magical, earth-shaking fuck. *Thank you, fuck-gods!* I silently whispered.

Outside, the hurricane seemed to have reached its maximum intensity – the wind was howling. Here in Alex's room, I may have howled a bit, too. Well, if I did and others in the hotel heard it, I'm sure they just thought, *Wow! That wind sounds really wild out there!* I smiled at the thought.

As we lay there, resting, I gradually became aware that Alex's stiff dick was still inside my pussy and was not finished with the little game we'd been playing. I knew that because every few seconds he would grasp me by my hips and lift me up slightly, then slide me slowly back down his flagpole, sending shudders throughout my body as my now super-sensitive pussy twerked and jerked.

And then he flipped me over. Well, flipped both of us over, to be more accurate. He just put one hand on my back and the other on my ass and rolled the both of us over – his cock never losing its place in my pussy – so that I was now on the bottom and he was on top, smiling down at me. Alex had smiled a lot this evening and I liked that. It meant he was having a good time.

He began sliding his cock in and out of me like a slow-moving piston in an idling engine, and as he did so, he talked to me. "You know, Jen, you're my dream girl," he told me. "Beautiful, soft, warm and cuddly, my perfect girl. I couldn't believe it when I met you. You looked exactly like the girl of my fantasies, the one I see in my dreams at night."

Oh, talk to me, Alex, talk to me! Talk to me some more!

And he did. "I've never understood what guys see in those skinny, bony, model-types who look like young boys – no ass, no tits, no meat at all," he explained. "I like girls with meat on their bones. Like you, Jennifer. You're perfect!"

Oh, oh, oh! Here we go again! I wasn't sure if it was the sweet-talk Alex was laying on me or the fact that, as he'd been talking, he'd been gradually increasing the speed of those piston strokes until his engine was now running at full power, but I came again. I reached up and grabbed his ass with both hands and pulled him tight against me and bucked my way to another amazing orgasm. I definitely felt like a slut now!

Alex's dick was amazing. It just never went soft. Over the next two hours, we exhausted all the positions I'd ever heard of and some I hadn't. I had a new orgasm – sometimes several – each time we changed positions. We went through *missionary, standing, kneeling, the bicycle kick, doggy-style, the back-breaker,* and several others that apparently have yet to be named. Alex came twice more and I came 6,241 times. Or thereabouts.

Two hours later, we were fucked out. We'd fucked ourselves silly. I'd used that expression before, of course, but I didn't know you could actually do it – fuck yourself or your partner silly. That's what happened, though. Every time Alex's hand or mouth or dick got near my pussy, I began to giggle. And every time I reached for his cock, he'd pull away, laugh and say,"No, no, I can't stand it anymore. It's too sensitive!" And then we'd both laugh. We'd fucked each other silly – literally!

I rather liked that expression. *Fucked me silly* was so much nicer than some other expressions that came to mind. Like *pounded my pussy to pieces* or *fucked my brains out!* While I do enjoy a good fuck, I'm not willing to risk my brains for one. And I certainly don't want my pussy pounded to pieces. Or to any other uncomfortable-sounding result, for that matter. But getting fucked silly is just fine.

At some point, we fell asleep. Or, at least, I did. The next thing I knew, Alex was sitting on the side of the bed, fully clothed, and was kissing me awake. "Umm," I said.

"I've got some bad news for you," he said.

OH, NO! HE'S MARRIED! shouted that little voice inside my head. I sat up, instantly awake. "What? What is it?"

He seemed amused by my reaction. "Well, it's not *that* bad," he said. "I have to leave."

"Leave? Now? Where are you going? What time is it, anyway?"

Alex laughed. "Wow! So many questions. Let's see. I have to go home. It's a company emergency. It's almost seven, the storm's gone and the airport has reopened. My plane is waiting for me."

"*Your* plane?"

"Yeah."

"To take you home? Back to Colombia?"

"Uh-huh."

"Will I see you again?"

He laughed. "Of course, silly, I'm going to be living here. But for now, I'll be back later this afternoon. Evening at the latest."

"You can do that? Go to Colombia and get back by evening?"

"Sure. It's my private jet. It takes off when I'm ready, when I tell it to."

"But Colombia is so far away," I said.

"It's not that far. Just a couple of states."

"What? What did you say?"

"South Carolina is just two states north of here. A couple of hours on my plane. I'll zip on up there, take care of business and be back before you know it."

South Carolina? Columbia, South Carolina? I began to laugh. No wonder they didn't have accents. I laughed harder.

"Are you okay?" The look on Alex's face was a mixture of amusement and concern. "What's so funny, anyways?"

I waited until I'd calmed down to an occasional giggle, then told him, "I'll explain it to you later."

"Okay, I guess," he said, looking totally confused.

"I guess I better get dressed and ready to go," I said.

"No, no, don't go. Stay here and wait for me until I get back. Take advantage of the hotel – the restaurant is great, there's a gym, all kinds of stuff. I'll be back as soon as I can."

"Won't the hotel be, uh, upset with me doing things like that? I'm not a guest."

"Well, you're *my* guest. I'll let them know you'll be staying until I return. And if anyone gives you a hard time while I'm gone, you just let me know and I'll fire them. All right?"

"*You'll* fire them?"

"Yeah. It's my hotel and if employees don't do what they're told, they get fired. That's how it works."

"*Your* hotel?"

"Well, technically it belongs to my company, but I own the company, so ..."

My head was spinning. Private planes, a guy with his own hotel, it was all a little hard to believe. "*You* own this hotel? You, or your company – whatever – *you* own it?"

He was grinning. "Sure. Haven't you noticed how nice the staff treats me? Yes, Mr. Entavez. Right away, Mr. Entavez. You want lobster rolls? Coming right up, Mr. Entavez."

Well, actually, I *had* noticed that. "Are you in the hotel business, then?" I said.

"No, no," he said, laughing. "It's computers. Cloud computing, to be more accurate. It's kinda complicated, but I'm in the process of moving my business down here. I have almost 500 employees and quite a few of them have to travel back and forth between Columbia and here, sometimes spending a week or more at a time down here, helping to set up the business. So I bought the hotel to make it easy for them. They stay here for free when they're in town."

"I see," I said. Alex's company sounded like a great place to work.

"I've gotta go, Jen," he said, kissing me again. "Will you wait for me?"

Oh, yeah! I'll definitely wait for you, Alex. I nodded. "I will," I told him.

"Great! I'll tell the staff you're my special guest. Anything you want, just ask. I'll be back before you can miss me." And with that and one more quick kiss, he was out the door.

I lay back and thought about all that had happened since Alex called me yesterday. This had to be the bestest-in-the-whole-wide-world one-night stand *ever*! And now it appeared he wanted it to be more than just a one-nighter. That was certainly all right with me!

I wished all this had happened to me a few nights earlier, back before I ordered the ten-inch monster dong with the clit-teasing and butt-fucking extensions and six vibrating speeds. I had the feeling that, with Alex around, I probably wasn't going to get much use out of that and the one hundred and nineteen dollars plus another eight bucks for expedited shipping I'd paid was wasted.

Unless ...

Marlene's birthday was coming up soon, and every year a bunch of us girls got together for a little celebration. Just six or eight of us, usually, out for dinner and then over to someone's house for drinks and outrageous stories, most of them bullshit. Maybe I'll just wrap that imitation schlong up real fancy and give it to Marlene as a birthday present.

I could almost see the surprised look on her face and hear her saying, "Fuck, Jen! Is this for real? This thing will split me wide open!" and me saying, "Practice, Marlene. Practice and you'll learn to love it!" and me and the rest of the girls all laughing.

Well, that solved that little problem. And for now, at least, things couldn't be better. I closed my eyes and went back to sleep, and though I can't be sure, I'd be willing to bet there was a smile on my face as I slept.

the end – fini – owari

Hey! Get your hand out of your crotch! This story's over. But there are lots more of my stories about horny young men and juicy young women available at your favorite online bookstore. Check them out, and while you're at it, please leave a (hopefully favorable) review. If you do, I'll write more stories, just for you.

In the meantime, here's a sample from Book 2 of the <u>Pleasantly Plump</u> series, as well as samples from Book 1 of my ongoing <u>Mike and Melanie</u> series and Book 1 of my ongoing <u>Waikiki Hummer</u> series. Hope you like them.

Pleasantly Plump 2 – Belinda's Story (Sample)

"**I** can't believe I let him do that to me," Harper was saying. "Shave my pussy, I mean."

Daisy started giggling and said, "Shh! People will hear you."

"Honestly, Harper, you're terrible," I said, shaking my head and acting shocked, although the keyword here is 'acting.' I wasn't really shocked at all. Envious, maybe. But not shocked.

We'd met at the gym. Just a bunch of girls trying to lose five or ten pounds so we'd be *perfect*. And then one day one of us – I don't remember who, it might even have been me – turned to the others and said, "Fuck this! I'm in the mood for a piece of cake. Anyone with me?" And that was the end of going to the gym for me, Daisy, Harper, and Mia. All four of us replaced our gym workouts with what we jokingly called our 'weekly cake-eaters club.'

But now there were only three of us. Mia had left *the club* to return to the gym after she gained 13 pounds in the first three weeks of cake-eating. The rest of us were good, though. A piece of cake and some coffee once a week hadn't caused us to gain any weight. We were still the sweet, pleasantly plump young women we'd always been. Okay, maybe change that word 'sweet' to 'nasty,' based on the story Harper was telling Daisy and me.

Harper was our resident slut, a girl who apparently had never met a cock she wasn't willing to suck and fuck and then tell the rest of us about it in great detail. Older than Daisy and me by about five years, she was divorced twice and living quite comfortably off the settlements from those divorces. She was tall, classy-looking, and always well-dressed. You'd never guess by looking at her that she was a first class cock-hound.

Daisy claimed she was named after some hot babe on an 80s TV show who always wore short – *really* short – cut-off jeans and skimpy tops, so she dressed like that. She looked like the slut that Harper actually was, but if some guy asked her if she wanted to hook up, she was more likely to break out in a giggle fit than to take him up on it.

And then there was me. Belinda. Who hadn't been laid in … well, so long I couldn't remember the last time. Even though I was, by many accounts, pretty hot. But for some reason, I just wasn't getting any action in the pussy-poking department.

"You gotta loosen up, Bee," was Harper's advice. "Stop looking for the perfect guy. There aren't any."

"Yeah, I know. But, …"

"But what?"

"All the guys I meet just want to fuck me two or three times and then move on. That's not what I'm looking for."

"So? What *are* you looking for?"

"That's just it. I'm not really sure. Something steady, I guess. A boyfriend."

Harper snorted. "Not the way to do it, in my opinion. Play the field. There are lots of guys out there to sample. Look, if you want, I can hook you up with 20 guys who'd be happy to fuck your brains out. All you'd have to do would be give 'em a call and say, "Busy?" and they'd come running. "You could be sucking and fucking a different dick every night of the week."

Daisy giggled and looked around the coffee shop, apparently worried someone might be overhearing our conversation.

"Yeah, but …" I said.

"But nothing! Just pick a guy who appeals to you and pick him up. It's easy."

"I wouldn't know what to say. Besides, guys are supposed to do the picking up, aren't they?"

"Shit, Bee, get with the program. It's the twenty-first century. You see something you want, you go after it."

"Well, maybe I'll give it a try sometime."

"Why sometime? Why not today? Why not now?"

"Now?"

"Sure. There are good-looking guys in here right now. Look around. See that guy behind the counter? That's Ted. I fucked him a couple of times – he's got a dick that would put a horse to shame!"

Daisy giggled some more and I acted shocked. "Ted? You fucked Ted? The guy who always makes sure we get extra-large pieces of cake?"

"Yeah. Why do you think he's always so happy to see us?"

"Ted? Really? I always thought he was gay."

"Not by a long shot," Harper said. She took a bite of her chocolate cake and gazed around the room, which was only about a quarter full. "See that guy over there? The tall guy with the crutches who for the past couple of minutes has been trying to figure out how to get his drink over to a table? He's been checking us out – I saw him. Why don't you go over and help him?"

I glanced in the direction Harper had indicated and, sure enough, a tall guy on crutches was hobbling over to a table, trying not to spill his coffee. He saw me looking at him and smiled in my direction. I quickly looked away.

"Crap! He caught me looking at him," I said.

"So what? Just go over there and tell him you're a cock polisher and ask him if he'd like to have his cock polished," Harper said with a leer. "I'll bet he says yes."

Daisy giggled extra hard at that and said, "Maybe you won't have to go over there. It looks like he's coming over here."

"He's coming to get *you*, Bee," Harper said.

"Stop it," I said, stealing a glance in crutches-guy's direction. Sure enough, he was heading our way. Slowly.

When he got to our table, he stopped, balancing on his right foot and his crutches. His left foot and lower leg were encased in a large, white cast, which he held up in the air. "Hi," he said.

We all said hi and looked at him expectantly. *Your move, buddy boy. Let's see what you've got.*

He turned directly to me and said, "I know this is going to sound like the oldest pickup line in the world, but don't I know you?"

Daisy giggled.

Harper stifled a laugh.

I looked up at him. He was really tall and he did look vaguely familiar. "I don't know. Do you?"

"West Valley High? Maybe like, about eight years ago? It's, uh, ... Belinda, isn't it?"

I took a closer look. Tall, slender, shaggy brown hair, good-looking, with a big, kinda goofy-looking grin revealing beautiful, straight, super-white teeth. Crowns, probably, but I've always found very white teeth to be extremely attractive. "Are you ... Danny Metters?" I said.

"Yeah, that's me," he said, wobbling dangerously on his crutches.

I couldn't believe it. Danny Metters was the biggest jock at West Valley High School when I was a student there. Quarterback of the football team, star forward on the basketball team – you know the type. But he was two years ahead of me in school and we never knew each other back then.

"Why don't you sit down?" Daisy said, pulling out a chair.

"Yeah. Before you fall down," Harper added, but in a humorous way – not mean.

Danny Metters flopped his long, lanky frame into the chair offered by Daisy, said, "Thanks," and laid his crutches on the floor.

"I'll go get your drink." Daisy said, and proceeded to retrieve the coffee he'd left on another table.

"This is a little hard to believe," I said to Danny. "How do you even know my name? We didn't know each other in school."

"Well, actually, I knew who you were," he said.

"Really? How?"

"You probably don't remember this but once I helped you pick up a bunch of books you dropped in the hall."

"Oh! I do remember that. Some jerk bumped into me and made me drop all my books and stuff and you stopped to help me."

"That's right."

"But that was, like, a 20-second encounter. And I was all flustered because you were this big shot sports hero and I was ... well, nobody. And you remember me from that? I'm surprised."

"Not that surprising, really. I made it a point to find out who you were after that. I was debating whether or not to ask you out, wondering if you'd say yes."

"What?!!"

"Yeah, I was going to ask you for a date."

I could feel myself blushing. "Why didn't you?"

"I broke my right ankle in a pickup basketball game, and I had this huge, dorky-looking cast on it for months. I couldn't drive, I couldn't dance, I couldn't do anything. And then it was graduation and off to college. I just never got around to it – I ran out of time."

"Is that what happened this time?" Harper said, pointing at the cast on his leg. "Basketball?"

"Actually, yes. I've been playing in China, in the Chinese Basketball League, for the past three years, but I tore my Achilles tendon a couple of months ago and I came back to the States to have surgery and get it fixed. Now I'm just waiting to get this cast off and start rehab."

"Ooh, a pro. Right?" said Harper.

"Uh-huh. The CBA is the major pro league in China."

"So what are you doing in Boca Raton?" I said. "You're a long way from home. Don't they have any good surgeons in the Bay Area?"

"Yeah, they do. In fact, I had the surgery performed in San Francisco last month." He paused, taking a drink of his coffee, then continued. "You remember Ozzie Bentz?"

I shook my head. "I don't think so."

"He was the basketball coach at West Valley – I played for him. And now he's the head coach at ACIUBR – Atlantic Coast International University of Boca Raton. And I'm his newest assistant coach. I contacted him a couple of months ago, while I was still in China, and he offered me a job. Sight unseen. But of course, he knows me, so …"

"Wow! Congratulations," I told him. "Then, no more China?"

"Nope. I'm looking for a place here. My pro career is over."

It was at about this time that I remembered my manners and introduced my two cake-eating compatriots to Danny. To be perfectly truthful, I hadn't thought about him in years but, back in high school, I used to think about him a *lot!* Especially after that time in the hallway.

"Can I ask you a question?" Harper said.

"Sure."

"Just how fucking tall are you, anyway?"

I blanched at Harper's choice of words and Daisy, right on cue, giggled. But Danny appeared not to even notice. He smiled at Harper and said, "In the basketball world, I'm six-eight. But in the real world, I'm about six-six."

"That's pretty tall," Daisy said, and Harper and I nodded in agreement.

"So, what about you?" Danny asked me. "What are you doing here, in Boca?"

"Well, I work for this company – Barrel Bottom Games – that used to be located in Hayward, but about a year ago, they decided the Bay Area was too expensive. So they relocated here and I came with them."

"That's a long way to move for a job."

"Not as far as moving from China, though."

He laughed. "You're right about that."

"Besides, it's my dream job."

"Yeah? What do you do?"

"I'm an animator. A junior animator, actually."

"Sounds like a cool job."

"I like it."

We spent the next 20 minutes rehashing old times – none of which we shared – in the East Bay, pretty much ignoring Harper and Daisy. And then Danny announced that he had to leave. It was time for a doctor's appointment. He retrieved his crutches from the floor and wobbled to his feet.

"I'm glad I bumped into you," he told me.

"Me, too."

"How do you get around?" Harper said. "With that cast on your foot – can you drive?"

"Well, I can. But it's awkward. This cast takes up so much room. So I hired a guy to drive me around." He turned and nodded toward another tall guy, down at the other end of the shop, who was busy chatting up a couple of girls. "Him. It's a good thing, too. I'd never find my way around this town. It's really confusing."

Harper, Daisy and I all agreed with that.

"So, look," Danny said. "How about we get together one of these nights, have a couple of drinks? We could go on that high school date that never happened."

I glanced over at Harper. A huge grin was spreading across her face and she nodded slightly at me, as if to say, "Go for it!"

"Sure, I'd like that. Sounds like fun."

We swapped phone numbers and he left, saying, "I'll call you and we'll set something up."

"Great," I said, and watched him hobble his way out.

"He's really tall," Harper said, after Danny had left. "I'll bet he's got a big dick."

Daisy giggled and I said, "Damn, Harper! Is that all you ever think about? Dicks?"

"Pretty much," she said, grinning. "Big, juicy dicks."

"Dicks aren't juicy," Daisy observed. "Pussies are juicy." And then she giggled again.

"Whatever. Based on my observations, the bigger the guy, the bigger the dick. And I've seen a lot of them. I'll bet your friend Danny has a monster inside those pants."

"That's not always true," Daisy said. She lowered her voice to a whisper, leaned forward and said, "I fucked this little short guy once and he had the biggest dick I've ever seen. Must have been almost a foot long when it was hard."

"Ooh, that sounds yummy!" Harper said. "I like 'em big."

"Me, too," Daisy agreed, and then they both looked at me.

"What?" I said.

"How about you?" Harper said. "You like 'em big? Those big, *monster* cocks?"

I thought about it. "I don't know. I don't think I've ever seen a cock you could describe as a *monster*. Except in porno videos. But never in person."

"They're the best. Big, long, fat stiffies that give you that filled-up feeling," she said, and Daisy nodded in agreement with Harper's assessment of big cocks, saying, "Yup. Yup."

"I guess I'll have to take your word for it," I said. "Anyway, I've gotta go. I've got some shopping to do." I stood up. "Same time next week?"

They both nodded.

"See ya then," I said, and left.

And that's the end of this sample. Darn! Just when things were starting to get interesting for Belinda, too. I wonder what's going to happen. Do you think reconnecting with an old high school fantasy will lead somewhere? It's

possible, I guess, but you know what they say – the fantasy is always better than the reality. Is that true? The only way to know for sure is to download the book.

Here's another sample for you. This one is from my <u>Mike and Melanie Escapades</u> series, an examination into the swinging lifestyle of a young, unmarried couple in their twenties. I like to think of these stories as <u>non-stop nasty!</u> I'll bet you'll agree.

Valentine Surprise: A Mike and Melanie Escapade, Book 1

"We'll meet in the bedroom at nine o'clock, okay? But you have to be in there 15 minutes early. And no peeking out."

"Sounds like a plan," Mike said. "I'll be there, waiting for my surprise."

"You're gonna like this one, I promise," I told him.

"I always like your surprises, Mel. You know that."

"Yeah, but this is gonna be the best one ever. By far!"

He laughed at my enthusiasm and went back to watching the news on TV. I started fixing dinner while I thought about how Mike would react to his 'surprise.' Surprises were a fun game Mike and I had been playing for the past year or so. Usually they were just little sex things, like an extra-sloppy blowjob for Mike. Or like the time he bought me an eight-inch long, extra-thick, silicone dildo and then fucked me with it. But I had something special planned for this evening, something that had taken me a lot of effort to arrange. My college roommate and long-time friend, Susan, was coming over to help me treat Mike to a Valentine's Day surprise – a threesome.

It had taken a bit of arm-twisting to get her to agree. Well, ... not really, now that I think about it. In fact, I think the first time I brought it up she said something like, "Mike? You mean, your hunky old man with the big dick?"

And I said, "He's not old. He's 28. And how do you know how big his dick is?"

"You told me."

"Oh, yeah. I guess I did mention he has a nice, big dick."

"About 40 times."

I stuck my tongue out at her. "So, how about it?"

"Sure. He's a hunk. I've always wanted to fuck Mike – I've told you so." That she had. It was the reason I'd been confident Susie would agree to my plans for a threesome. And so we'd made plans to double-team him on Valentine's Day.

They called her 'Susie the Slut' back when we were in school, a nickname she well-deserved. She was a pretty blonde with big, natural boobs, a nice round ass and a really *friendly* attitude toward dicks. We weren't exactly roommates – we shared a two-bedroom apartment off campus. I had my own bedroom and Susie had hers, and hers had frequent visitors. *Lots* of them!

But that was then and this is now. And tonight, Susie was going to be the visitor. I had my fingers mentally crossed that everything would work out the way we'd planned it.

After dinner, Mike went into the den to do something on the computer. Watch porn, probably. That was good preparation for the evening's upcoming activities, I thought. *Get nice and horny, Mike. Susie the Slut and I are going to screw you silly!*

I took control of the TV and spent some time channel surfing but was unable to find anything that interested me. Other things were on my mind. I was worried that Susie might not show up on time or, worse yet, might not show up at all. And as the clock inched closer to ten to nine, the time she was supposed to arrive, my apprehension grew.

At quarter to nine, Mike kissed me on the forehead, said, "I'll be waiting," then disappeared into the bedroom and closed the door. At least step one was going off on schedule, I thought. That was a good omen.

Ten to nine came and went. And no Susie. I wondered if I should call her and see what happened, but while I was thinking about it, my doorbell rang. I breathed a sigh of relief and padded to the door. "I was starting to get worried," I said as I opened the door.

Only, it wasn't Susie standing there on my front porch. Well, that's not right – she *was* there. But she wasn't alone. There was a guy on the porch with her.

"You brought a date?!!" I said.

"Not exactly. I showed up alone, but he was already here."

"I looked more closely at the guy standing next to her. "Jerry?"

"Hi, Mel," he said.

"What are you doing here?" Jerry was Mike's basketball buddy. The two of them played almost every Sunday afternoon in pickup games at a church gym where Jerry was a part-time custodian. He was something of a stud, tall and muscular and rumored to have a giant-sized cock, and I'd fantasized about fucking him more than a few times.

"Uh, Mike asked me to come over. Something about a ... a surprise." Even in the dim light on the porch, I could see Jerry was blushing – he obviously knew more about the 'surprise' than he was letting on.

I almost burst out laughing as it suddenly dawned on me what was happening – Mike had seen me flirting with Jerry a couple of times and had decided to set us up, as his surprise for me. "Come in, come in," I said.

The three of us settled into the living room. "You two know each other?" I asked Susie.

"We met on your front porch, Mel. So, ... yeah, we've met."

"Okay, let me go get Mike. Be right back." I left to inform Mike of what was happening.

He was lying on the bed, watching TV. "Is it time?" he said.

"Change of plans. We've got company."

He grinned, obviously knowing Jerry was scheduled to appear. "Really? What happened?"

"Come out into the living room and see," I said, turning to leave. "I'm gonna make drinks."

"Break out that wine I bought last week."

"Yeah, okay." I went back to the living room, where Susie and Jerry had made themselves comfortable on our sofa. "Drinks?" I said and, without waiting for an answer, proceeded to open the pinot noir Mike had requested.

Mike came padding out of the bedroom, saying, "Hi, guys," and joining us. He didn't seem surprised to see Susie and, of course, he knew Mike would be there since he'd invited him.

"See that bowl on the coffee table? The marbly one?" I said to Susie.

"Yeah."

"Open it."

She pulled the top off the bowl and peered inside. "Hey, weed! And some of it is all rolled up, ready to go. Great."

"Yeah, light a couple,"I told her. "There are lighters in that other bowl."

Susie torched a couple of joints and sent one down the sofa for me to share with Mike, who was sitting on the floor, on a *zabuton*. We sat smoking and sipping our wine for a while, not really talking much. The situation was awkward. We all knew why we were here, together – at least, we all knew to some degree – but none of us seemed to know how to get things started and conversation was on the light side.

"This is nice," Jerry said. "This weed, I mean. It's nice and smooth, not harsh. I like it."

"Yeah, I bought it last week," Mike said. "It's called *Beautiful Dream*." We all agreed it was 'nice.' And then the conversation lagged again.

Eventually, Mike said to me, "By the way, whatever happened to that big surprise you promised me? It's long after nine o'clock. Almost ten."

I took a big hit off the joint, held it for a few seconds, then blew it out in the direction of Susie. "It's sitting right there," I said, pointing at her.

Susie flashed a big grin at Mike and said, "Hel-lo, Mike, my man. Surprise, surprise. Why don't you come up here and sit next to me?" She stood up and swapped places with me, telling me to, "Scoot over there, next to Jerry."

So I moved over, close to Jerry. Real close. And when I looked back, Mike was already sitting on the sofa and Susie was straddling his lap, sucking his face and giving him a little bit of a reverse lap-dance. That was quick! Leave it to Susie to get this train rolling.

"Looks like they're having fun," Jerry said.

I watched them for a few seconds. "Yeah, that does look like fun," I agreed. I leaned up and kissed him, at the same time dropping my hand into his lap, not really surprised to find something hard hiding inside his shorts.

"Hey, I'm going to give Susie a tour of the house," Mike suddenly announced, temporarily interrupting my attempt to get something going with Jerry.

"Fine," I told him. "Make sure you show her the bedroom."

"Oh, I will. Don't worry." The two of them headed off in the direction of our bedroom, and I went back to what I'd been doing – kissing Jerry. So maybe Mike's threesome wasn't going to work out tonight. But I was sure he wasn't going to be disappointed. Susie had lots of experience and I was sure Mike was going to have a good time.

And I was going to have a good time, too. At least, I hoped so. I broke my kiss with Jerry and said, "Mike told me you have a king-sized cock. Is that true?"

He looked embarrassed. "It's, ... uh, yeah, it's pretty big."

"Can I see?"

"If you want to."

"Oh, I do," I said, smiling at him. "I definitely do."

"Help yourself," he said.

I unbuttoned the front of his shorts, which were tenting big time, and unzipped his fly. "Something big is in there," I said, stating the obvious.

He didn't say anything, he just grinned.

I reached in and pulled it out. Ever heard the term, *monster dick*? That's what popped out of Jerry's pants – a humongous monster of a dick. It looked delicious. I stroked it slowly up and down with one hand. It wasn't only long, it was thick. "Damn, Jerry, that's a big one!" I said.

And that's the end of the sample of <u>Valentine Surprise: A Mike and Melanie Escapade, Book 1</u>. *I wonder what Mel's going to do, now that Jerry's monster has been released from its cage. I have a pretty good idea but I don't want to give the fun away. You can find out by downloading the book and reading it.*

Wait, wait, don't go. There's one more sample and it's a good one. It's from <u>The Waikiki Hummer</u>, *the first book in my* <u>Waikiki Hummer</u> *series. Not every erotic story is a romance, and the stories in this series are about as far from romances as you can get. Even so, the ongoing adventures of Terry Jean Rollins, a young Waikiki woman who likes to hum while performing oral sex, are guaranteed to bring forth a* <u>damp</u> *feeling in female readers or a big old* <u>stiffy</u> *in males. I usually describe these stories as erotic-mystery-revenge-thriller-adventure, sort of. They are definitely NOT romances!*

The Waikiki Hummer (Sample)
A Waikiki Hummer Adventure – Book 1

Foreword

Terry Jean Rollins – TJ to her friends and The Waikiki Hummer to the rest of the world – is a cute, blonde, 23-year-old resident of Waikiki with only one ambition in life, to suck the cocks of as many shy, middle-aged, dorky male visitors to Waikiki as she can. She is a self-confessed dork lover who considers herself to be "maybe the best cocksucker in the entire world!" and dick-draining dorky tourists is her hobby. These are her stories, every one of them 110% true, according to her.

ONE

He was sitting in the center section of the bus, alone, leaning against the window, looking sad and forlorn, wearing horned-rim glasses and a really dorky-looking crew cut. *And,* there was a wedding ring on his finger. Perfect. Just what I was looking for.

Probably on his way to Ala Moana Center, I judged as I walked down the aisle toward him. When I got there, I said, "Mind if I sit next to you?" and flashed my friendliest smile.

He scooted over to give me more room, probably thinking it was odd I chose to sit next to him, since the bus was practically empty. But he said, "Fine," and smiled back at me.

I slid in beside him. "Here on vacation?" I said.

"Business. You?"

"I live here," I said.

"Lucky you." The way he said it made it sound as though his visit to Honolulu had so far been less than pleasurable. Given the chance, I hoped to change all that for him.

"Where you from?"

"Colorado. Denver."

"It sounds like you're not enjoying yourself here in our beautiful city."

"It's all right."

"How about your wife?" I pointed at his wedding ring. "I'll bet she likes it."

"She's not here. It's just me. Here on business."

Excellent! "How long is it, anyway?" I said.

He gave me a funny look. "What?"

"How long? Your business trip?"

"Oh. Two weeks. One more to go." He repeated the look. I couldn't quite tell what it meant. Apprehension, perhaps? Or maybe lust. I am, after all, not *that* bad looking. I wouldn't describe myself as beautiful –

cute would probably be a better description. I've heard guys call me that. "She's a really cute girl," they'd say. And I think I agree with them. I *am* cute. I've got perky tits and a nice round ass and a really *friendly*-looking smile.

"I'm TJ," I said, and offered my hand.

"George," he said, shaking it with a slightly-damp palm.

When he released my hand, I let it drop down and land on his left thigh, just a few inches from his lap. He flinched slightly but left it there. I gave his thigh a tiny, almost-imperceptible squeeze.

"What do you like to do for excitement. George? What turns you on?" I flashed him that friendly smile once again.

"I play chess."

Excitement? Chess? That wasn't the kind of answer I'd been expecting.

"And golf. I'm a really good golfer."

Ooh, more excitement. "Really?"

"Yup. I've even won a couple of tournaments."

"You don't say." I gave his thigh another squeeze – a little harder this time – and slid my hand a couple of inches closer to his crotch. He looked down at it but didn't complain.

"What about you, TJ?"

"Me?"

"Yeah. What do you do for excitement? What are your hobbies?"

This conversation wasn't heading in the direction I'd intended. My new friend, George, seemed to be a little slow on the uptake. I decided I needed to be more direct. "I only have one hobby," I told him.

"And? What is it?"

I turned and leaned closer to him and put my mouth up close to his ear. Then, in my best sexy-sounding voice, I whispered, "I like to suck cock." As I said it, I switched hands on his thigh and slid my left hand the rest of the way up his thigh, into his crotch, and grabbed his cock through his pants. Surprise, surprise – it was already rock-hard. Maybe George wasn't as slow as he seemed.

His eyebrows shot up about 14 inches. "What?" he said, turning to look at me.

"I like to pick up strange men – almost always tourists – and go to their hotel with them and then give them the best blowjob they've ever had in their entire life. It's my specialty. Blowjobs." I smiled and squeezed his cock several more times.

"How much?" George said.

"What?" I didn't understand the question.

"How much do you charge?"

I pulled my head back and gave him my best *disappointed* look. "Really, George? You think I'm a hooker? Look at me. Look at how I'm dressed." My outfit of the day consisted of white shorts, a baby-blue T-shirt and rubber *zoris* instead of shoes.

"Have you seen the hookers in this town, George? They're cruising Waikiki every night, strolling up and down Kalakaua, asking tourists if they'd like a *date*. Their skirts are four inches long and the heels of their shoes are twice that."

"I've seen 'em." he said.

I squeezed his cock again – hard, this time – and didn't release it for several seconds. "It's a hobby with me, George. I just like sucking dick. It makes me feel ... oh, I don't know. Powerful, I guess." Yeah. Taking that stiff dick and turning it into a soft little lump of flesh with the consistency of a limp dishcloth, it makes me feel powerful.

"I see."

"And I especially like strange men."

"Strange? You think I'm strange?"

"Not strange weird. Strange like we don't know each other."

"Oh."

"So, ...?"

"No charge?"

"Nope."

"All right. I'm up for it," he said.

"Obviously," I said, pointing at his pants, which now featured a tent where the fly was. "You'd better carry something in front of that when we get off the bus."

"I'll do that." He smiled, picked his briefcase up off the floor and held it up for me to see.

"Perfect," I told him.

TWO

The hotel where George was staying was not one of the fancy, beachfront, super-expensive tourist traps fronting Kalakaua Avenue with back doors that open up right onto the beach. I guess I should have expected that, since George had said he was here on business, not as a tourist. Anyway, it was on a side street, almost three blocks up from the beach, near Ala Wai Boulevard and the canal.

We had to hail a cab after we got off the bus. George's hotel was back down at the other end of Waikiki, the Diamond Head end. The driver who stopped to pick us up wasn't too happy about the fact we were only going a few blocks but George promised him a big tip and when we got there, he gave him a twenty and told him to keep the change. The cabbie thanked us and drove off with an extra-large smile on his face.

George's room was on the ninth floor, with a view of Ala Wai Boulevard, Ala Wai Canal, and the Ala Wai Golf Course on the other side of the canal. With the exception of the lanai – which I doubted got much use because of the constant winds swirling around this area – it was just a standard hotel room like you might find in any business hotel in any large city. There was a double bed, a desk and chair, a dresser, an armchair, a medium-size flat-screen TV and, of course, a bathroom and a place to hang clothes. Nothing fancy, but then, we weren't here for the décor, anyway.

"What now?" George said, turning to face me.

"Why don't you take off some of those clothes? Honolulu's too hot to be wearing a suit."

"Yeah, you're right. It *is* hot." He started removing his clothes, tossing them onto the armchair while at the same time casting nervous glances in my direction.

"Relax, George," I told him, adding a slight chuckle. "I'm not going to hurt you. I'm not going to rob you or yell rape or anything like that. I just want to suck your cock. It's my hobby, it's what I do for fun."

"Strange hobby," he said.

He had stripped down to just his boxer shorts and socks by this time and was trying to remove his socks by hopping on one foot while he pulled a sock off the other foot. It wasn't going that well – he was hopping all over the room, trying to maintain his balance. When he hopped by me, I reached out and pushed him over backwards, onto the bed, and pulled off both socks for him.

"Thanks," he said, looking up at me from his recumbent position.

"Wouldn't want you to hurt yourself before we get to the fun part." I hopped up on the bed and slid up close to him, with my head on his right shoulder and my right arm draped over his chest. "Comfy?" I said.

"Uh-huh."

"Good." I stretched my head up and began to nibble on his right ear. At the same time my right hand slithered down his body until it landed on top of his once-again-rock-hard cock, but outside his boxer shorts. I let it rest there, separated from his dick by just a thin layer of cotton, without doing anything – no squeezing, no stroking, nothing – while I continued to chew on his ear.

He shivered.

"Relax, George. You're gonna like this. I promise."

"I think I already like it."

"It gets better," I said. I slipped my hand under the waistband of his shorts and wrapped my fingers around his dick, giving it a couple of light squeezes – what I like to think of as *introductory* squeezes or *How do you do?* squeezes.

George moaned and said, "Fuck, that feels good!"

"Take off your shorts," I told him.

He reached down and, with just a little help from me, slipped his boxers down over his hips and onto his legs, from where he kicked them off. His cock – six inches of thick, beautiful man-meat – stared up at me, wavering up and down, practically wearing a *Please hurry up and do me* sign. I smiled, thinking *that's what I'm here for,* leaned down and sucked that beautiful purple-headed shaft into my mouth.

George seemed to like that. I swirled my tongue slowly around the head of his dick, occasionally licking upward on the bottom of the shaft, only to concentrate again on the head. Any girl who's sucked a few cocks will tell you that's where the action is – the dickhead. The shaft is really only there so you'll have something to hang onto while you're working on the head.

Apparently, though, it had been a long while since George had been laid or gotten his dick gobbled, because I was just getting started, just warming up, when I felt his cock go super-hard and begin to spasm. I put my tongue on the bottom of his dickhead, wiggled it back and forth slowly, and began to gently suck.

A warm stream of cum – my tasty reward, as I usually liked to think of it – spurted out onto my tongue, followed by a slight pause and then two more spasmodic ejections. I sucked it all up and swallowed, never letting go of his dick. But it wasn't just George's dick doing the spasm thing. His whole body shook and he arched his back each time he pumped a load into my mouth. He commented out loud on it, too. He went, "Oh! Oh! Oh!' and "Oh!"

I spit his dick out into my hand and hung onto it, massaging it gently as I watched him gasping for air, trying to catch his breath. He really wasn't in the best of shape for a guy – what, forty or fifty years old? The thought crossed my mind I might have some explaining to do if old George had a heart attack and croaked on me.

"Shit! I'm so sorry," he said when he was able to breathe normally again.

"Don't worry about it," I said, laughing. "We're not finished yet."

"No?"

"No." Actually, this – getting a load of warm jizz shot into my mouth 20 seconds or so after I start sucking a strange guy's cock – happened to me a lot. But I was never disappointed. I liked to think it was because I was such a skillful cocksucker I could get any guy to cum in record time. And also, I knew we were just getting started. If George thought that shooting one little load of cum down my throat was the end of this adventure, he was in for a big, big surprise.

I've always thought of cocksucking as an art form, something to be done slowly and gracefully, leisurely, sensually stroking and licking your way toward a tasty treat until a stream of warm, delicious cum – the reward – fills your mouth and rolls down your throat. When done right, it can take hours, with the reward being repeated two and sometimes three times, until that poor, pitiful penis is completely wasted, of no good to any woman for several days. And that's what I intended to do to George – suck his cock so dry it would be useless for the next week or so!

THREE

I let George rest while I entertained myself playing with his dick and giving it an occasional wet, slurpy lick, just to keep him interested. When I was younger, I used to wish I was a boy so I'd have a dick to play with whenever I wanted, but as I got older I realized that wasn't necessary. Any reasonably decent-looking girl could pretty much find a cock to play with any time she wanted. Usually, all you had to do was ask.

After 15 or 20 minutes of me diddling with it, George's dick had re-inflated to a sort of floppy, spongy fullness – not really hard but on its way. During the entire time, he only said two things to me, "I like that," and "Are you for sale? I want to buy you and take you home with me." The rest of the time he just moaned.

I thought I knew a way to speed things up. I used my hand to milk his cock for a minute or two, then leaned over, put it in my mouth and began massaging the tip – just the top part of his dickhead – with my tongue. At the same time I began to hum.

"What the hell?" George propped himself up on both elbows and gazed at me, looking slightly alarmed. "What are you doing?"

I pulled his cock out of my mouth, making an exaggerated smacking sound as I did so. "Round two," I told him.

"No, I mean that noise. That buzzing sound. What was that?"

Keeping George's cock in my hand, I sat back on my haunches. "I was humming."

A puzzled look slid across his face, replacing the alarm. "Why?"

I shrugged. "I like it. It's my thing. I like to hum while I suck cock."

"You're kidding!"

"Nope." To prove it to him, I leaned forward, popped his dick back into my mouth, and hit him with about 20 seconds of the Australian folk song, *Waltzing Matilda*. When I spit his dick back out into my hand, it was quite a bit firmer than when it had gone in. Also larger. "See? Guys like it, too," I said.

"Is it always that song?" he asked me.

"Nope. I mix 'em up. Why? You got a favorite song you want me to hum for you?"

"Yeah. *In the Still of the Night*."

"Shit, how old *are* you, anyway? Damn, George, that song's like a hundred years old."

"I know, but I can't help it. I like fifties music. And that's one of my favorites. Do you know it?"

"The Five Satins, right?"

"Yeah."

"I think I do." I leaned back down and slurped his dick – still only at about half-mast but trying hard to make it up to the crow's nest – into my mouth, lightly sucking and tonguing the tip as I began to hum *In the Still of the Night*.

And then a funny thing happened. As I was working my tongue in a circular motion around the head of George's cock, humming his favorite song and forcing that cock into a more-rigid state, he began to sing along with me. Pretty loudly, in fact.

Trouble was, George wasn't much of a singer. In fact, he was fucking terrible! But I knew just the cure for that. I rolled over to one side and removed my shorts and panties, then climbed back on top of him. Temporarily abandoning his almost totally firmed-up dick for the moment, I crawled up his body until my crotch was about an inch from his face.

"You like pussy, George?" I asked him.

"I do."

"Take a good look, then. Freshly washed, carefully shaved, just a nice, clean, smooth, moist pussy, with no hair to get in your mouth and spoil that creamy goodness." I moved a little forward, grabbed him by the ears and gently pulled his head upward. Just a bit. Then I lowered my cunt – now juicy with anticipation – onto his waiting mouth, grinding it against his lips before releasing his ears and spreading open my pussy with my fingers to make sure his tongue would have easy access to my clit.

Oh, too bad. That's the end of this sample of The Waikiki Hummer, Book 1. *And just when things were starting to get interesting, too. TJ's time with George is almost up and she's about to get involved with Tony, a bad guy from the mainland who's definitely* not *her type. And when she* accidentally *ends up in possession of a large amount of counterfeit twenty-dollar bills, her life gets complicated. I don't want to give the rest of the story away – like I said, it's a good one. And it's available at your favorite online bookseller.*

Well, that's it. I hope you enjoyed the book and the free previews. If you haven't done so already, don't forget to leave a review for this book, Pleasantly Plump Book 1 – Jennifer's Story. *I'd sure appreciate it and if you do this for me, I will write more stories, just for you, and I will love you FOREVER!*

See ya soon, I hope! Shannon